Baldwin Public Library

WITHDRAWN

FEB 0 9 2007

P9-DGQ-882

Baldwinsville Public Library
33 East Genesee Street
Baldwinsville, NY 13027-2575

WITHDRAWN

Whoosh
WENT THE WIND!

written by **Sally Derby**

illustrated by **Vincent Nguyen**

Marshall Cavendish Children

Text copyright © 2006 by Sally Derby
Illustrations copyright © 2006 by Vincent Nguyen

Marshall Cavendish Corporation
99 White Plains Road
Tarrytown, NY 10591
www.marshallcavendish.us

Library of Congress Cataloging-in-Publication Data
Derby, Sally.
Whoosh Went the Wind! / by Sally Derby ; illustrated by Vincent Nguyen.— 1st ed.
p. cm.
Summary: A boy tries to convince his teacher that the reason he is late for school is that,
over and over, he had to undo the damage being caused by the wind, from tearing laundry
off the line to blowing away street signs.
ISBN-13: 978-0-7614-5309-3
ISBN-10: 0-7614-5309-1
[1. Winds—Fiction. 2. Teachers—Fiction. 3. Tall tales.] I. Nguyen, Vincent, ill. II. Title.
PZ7.D4416Who 2006
[E]—dc22
2005027582

FEB 0 9 2007

The text of this book is set in Calvert.
The illustrations are rendered in acrylic paint and charcoal pencil.
Book design by Adam Mietlowski

Printed in China
First edition

1 3 5 6 4 2

Marshall Cavendish
Children

With love to Steven, our dreamer
and Master of Enthusiasms
—S.D.

For Roberta Sadja and Jeff Markowsky,
whose class I was never late for
—V.N.

I'm late! I'm late, but it's not my fault.
I started for school in plenty of time, but the minute
I stepped outside, the wind whooshed over me. Oh,
how the wind was blowing. . . .

It snatched laundry from our clothesline and tangled it in the trees. I climbed tree after tree and tossed clothes down until, "Hurry," Mom said. "You'll be late."

You should have listened to her.

Oh, I did. I whizzed down the street while the wind zigzagged ahead, whisking dandelions out of the grass and heaping them in my way. The wind blew and the golden hill grew.

A hill of dandelions? Now, really. . .

It's true! I climbed that dandelion mountain, but then something fell at my feet. The post office flag was flapping so hard its stars fluttered down to the sidewalk. I picked up stars till my pockets were full, then, just as the clock struck eight, the wind blew open the doors of Milady's Millinery Shop.

Those heavy doors blew open? I find that hard to believe!

But they did! The wind huffed into the store and sent hats like flowered Frisbees sailing out the door. I ran and I jumped, I caught all that I could, till I held a hat bouquet.

I was taking them back inside when I heard a clatter and clang. Traffic signs began flying! The wind jumbled them, then dropped them in spots where they were never meant to be.

Flying traffic signs? You must be kidding me!

It's true, it really is! Cars stopped while drivers dithered, so I directed traffic until a policeman came. And still the wind kept blowing. It whirled away a picket fence and dropped the pieces on the Play Time Preschool playground.

I couldn't stay, so I hurried on, but as I ran past Dippy Deli, I heard people clapping and laughing. The wind had gathered all the strays in town and was nestling them among the groceries in people's shopping carts.

Free pets at Dippy Deli? Now you're going too far.

But it's true, and that's not all. . . . Five chickens and a rooster floated to town on the wings of that wandering wind. They clucked and squawked on the courthouse roof and ignored their farmer's calls. But I had popcorn in my lunch bag, so I scattered it around, and the chickens came flapping down.

You expect me to believe you just happened to have popcorn in your lunch bag?

It's true, I always do!

We caged up the chickens and I sped along, then, just as I cut through the park, the wind sighed a foggy breath. The fog grew deep, the park grew dark. Soon all I could see was gray. A ghostly figure loomed, and I shook with fright, but it turned out to be just the statue in the middle of Lion Fountain. So there was the fountain, but which way was OUT?

You're saying you were lost in a fog, lost on the way to school?

It's true, I was lost, till the wind caught its breath and blew away the fog. Then I sprinted along with wind in my face and wind in my hair and my shoes hardly touching the walk. What magic the wind was blowing! It banged a hundred screen doors all at once. It tolled the church bells upside down and sent the pigeons flying.

Then with a roar, the wind whooshed me up. I soared over roads and rooftops, I floated past towers and trees. Birds flapped beside me, clouds brushed my hair. And just when I thought I'd never get back, softly as a kitten's breath, it set me down . . . right by the school's front door.

I guess you don't believe me?

You're right, I don't believe you.

But it's true! It's all true!
Can't you hear the wind calling?
Just open the window and see.

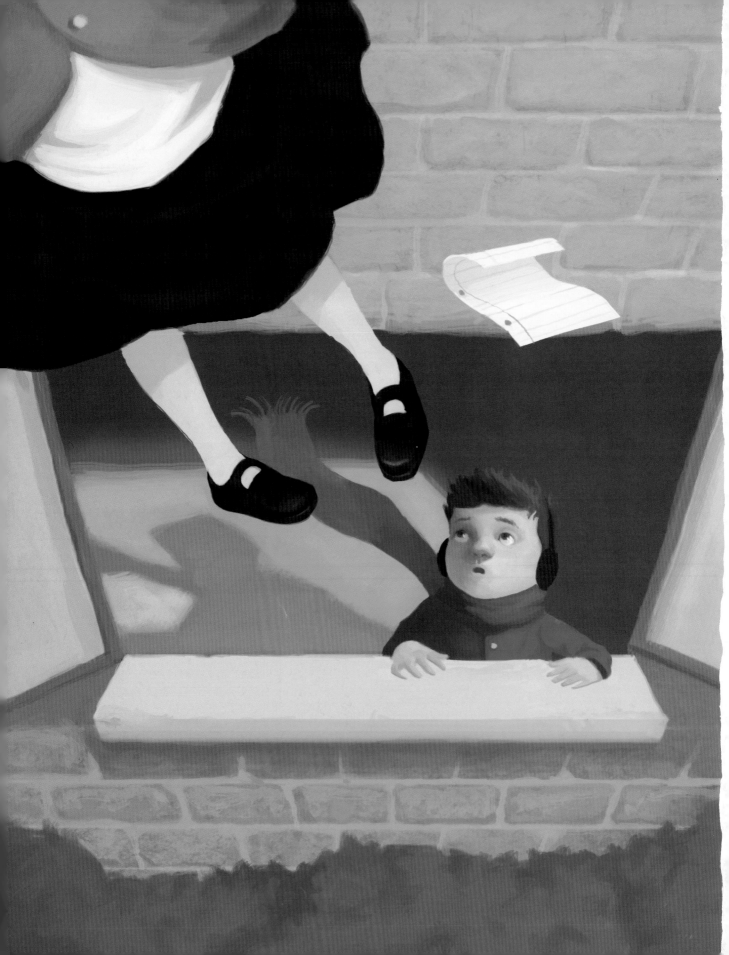